Who's Your Real Mom?

words

Bernadette Green

illustrations

Anna Zobel

For Lucinda and Uma, who know what
it's like to be asked 'Who's your real mom?' —*Bernadette*

For my own beautiful mom. —*Anna*

The illustrations in this book were made with ink and Copic marker, and layered digitally.

Typeset in Baskerville

Scribble, an imprint of Scribe Publications
18–20 Edward Street, Brunswick, Victoria 3056, Australia
2 John Street, Clerkenwell, London, WC1N 2ES, United Kingdom
3754 Pleasant Ave, Suite 100, Minneapolis, Minnesota 55409 USA

Text © Bernadette Green 2020
Illustrations © Anna Zobel 2020

First published by Scribble 2020

This book is printed with vegetable-soy based inks, on FSC® certified paper from responsibly managed forests and other controlled material, ensuring that the supply chain from forest to end-user is chain of custody certified. Printed and bound in China by 1010.

9781925849493 (Australian hardback)
9781912854868 (UK hardback)
9781913348137 (UK paperback)
9781950354245 (US hardback)

Catalogue records for this title are available from
the National Library of Australia and the British Library

scribblekidsbooks.com

'Elvi, which one is your mom?' asked Nicholas.

'They're both my mom.'

'But which one's your real mom?'

'I told you. They're both my real mom,' said Elvi.

'Only the one who had you in her tummy
can be your real mom,' said Nicholas. 'Which one is that?'

'Fine!' said Elvi. 'She's wearing jeans.'

Nicholas frowned. 'They're both in jeans.'

'She's got dark hair.'

'They both have dark hair. I need a clue.'

'She's got a scar above her eyebrow
that looks like a moon,' said Elvi.

Nicholas squinted. 'I can't see from here.
Give me a good clue.'

'She's the one who can do a handstand on one finger.'

'No one can do that,' scoffed Nicholas.

'My mom can.'

'Also, she's the one who can pull a car with her teeth.'

'Her teeth would break!' said Nicholas.

'No,' said Elvi, 'because actually,
they're reinforced with diamonds.'

'She's the one who's a pirate in disguise.

Her pockets are full of gold, and she has a parakeet
called Tony who stayed at home to look after our cat.

She speaks fluent gorilla. She regularly gets called to
the zoo to sort out gorilla disputes.'

'I went to the zoo last week!' said Nicholas.
'And I didn't see either of your moms. Give me a real clue.'

'My real mom crochets hammocks for polar bears,

can cartwheel up a mountain,

teaches spiders the
art of the web,

writes in a secret language
only whales can read,

calls her pelican friends when I want to go flying,

and can clip a dragon's toenails while
she's standing on her head *and*
eating a bowl of spaghetti.'

'Elvi! Just tell me who your real mom is!' Nicholas shouted.

'Okay,' said Elvi.

'She's the one who holds me when I'm scared.

She's the one who tucks me into bed.

And she's the one who kisses me goodnight.'

'Don't both your moms do that?' asked Nicholas.

ELVI

ELVI

'Exactly,' said Elvi.